The Band of Friends

Story retold by Michaela Morgan
Pictures by Nick Price

OXFORD
UNIVERSITY PRESS

Once upon a time, in a land not far away from here, there was a farm.

On that farm there were some:

Munch

Zzzz

contented cows,

Zzzz

dozy ducks,

Zzzz zzzz

lazy lambs and

Zzzz zzzz

Zzzz

sleepy sheep.

They all lived together happily. All they wanted was a quiet life.

On the same farm were

a donkey,

a dog,

a cat and

a rooster.

They were the best of friends and
had good fun together.

3

Best of all, this little band of animals **loved** to sing.

"I have never heard such a noise!" exclaimed the farmer.

"Everyone says that!" the donkey replied.

He was very proud of his loud voice.

Day after day the band of friends sang until the farmer could stand it no longer.

"Go away!" he shouted at the donkey, the dog, the cat and the rooster. "Go and make your noise somewhere else!"

"We could go away and sing somewhere else!" said the donkey. "We could become a famous pop group!"

"Good idea!" said the dog. "I'd like to be famous."

"We might even become rich," said the rooster.

They all imagined how wonderful that would be.

Then the cat sighed a little sigh and said, "Maybe we
could have our own little home, sing together
every night and live happily ever after.
That is what I would really like."

The animals set off on their adventure. As they went on their way, they sang their song and everyone they passed said,
    "What a noise!"

But the band of friends felt very proud of the music they made.

8

Down the long
dusty road they went.

Scritch scratch

Trot trot trot

Pitter pat pitter pat

Pad pad pad

On and on and on they
went, for mile after mile.

9

By the end of the day the animals were
        filthy,
                freezing,
                        famished
and very, very tired.

They stopped walking, they stopped singing and they sighed.
"I wish we had something to eat," groaned the dog.
"If only we had a warm fire," moaned the cat.
"We need a good roof over our heads,"
grumbled the rooster.

"What's that light in the woods? I think
I can see a cottage!" said the donkey,
and he trot trotted right up to it,
put his hoofs on the window
ledge and looked in.

11

"Oh!" sighed the donkey. "Look at that!"

"What is it?" asked the dog and he jumped up onto the donkey's back and then he peered through the window, too.

"Oh my!" he said.

"What is it?" asked the cat and she jumped up onto the dog's back so that she could see for herself. "Wonderful!" she sighed.

"What? What? What?" asked the rooster and he flew up and perched on the cat's head to get a bird's eye view.

This is what they saw:
 a cosy little room,
  a blazing log fire,
   a table piled high with delicious food and drink,
    some thick, warm rugs and soft, comfy chairs.

By the fire sat three big, bad robbers, counting their gold. They did not look at all friendly.

"They won't share with us," sighed the cat and she started to howl miserably.

"Miaoooooooooooooooooooow!" she howled.

The dog joined in "Wooooooooooooooooooooooo!" he wailed.

The donkey joined in with a "HEEEEEEEEE-HAAAAAW!"
The rooster joined in too.

"Cock a Dooooooooodle Dooooooooooooooooo."

"OOOOOOOOOOOOOOOOOOW!"

The robbers heard the noise
and they started to shake.

"This place is haunted!" said one of
the robbers.

He was shaking like a jelly. He
looked up at the window –

and this is what he saw.

He stopped shaking and he started screaming.

"AAAAAAAAAAAAAAAAAAAH!"

"OOOOOOOOOOOOOOOOOW!"

"What is it? What is it?" asked the other robbers. They all ran to the window. The four animals were perched one on top of the other. In the light of the moon, they looked like a horrible monster.

The first robber stopped screaming and started running. He ran out of the cottage, down the road and into the woods. He climbed a tree and hid in it. The other robbers followed him.

"OOOOOOOOOOOOOOOW!"

"They've left the cottage for us!" said the donkey. "Let's go in!"
The four friends went inside.

First they ate the food.
Gobble, gobble, gulp and *slurp.*
They ate until they could eat no more. It was delicious.

Then they drank the milk.
Lick lick lap and *lick,*
   slurp, slurp, burp.
They drank until they could drink no more. It was refreshing.

Then, one by one, they found a comfy place and
settled down to sleep in the warm, cosy cottage.

The donkey lay across the doorway. The cat curled
up by the fire. The dog dozed on a big, soft chair, and
the rooster roosted in the roof. They fell fast asleep.

Meanwhile, in the wood, the robbers were still hiding in a tree but now they had stopped shivering and shaking.

The biggest robber spoke. "I'm going back to the cottage," he said. "I'll check to see if it's safe now. Then you can follow me."

He scrambled down from the tree and tip-toed back to the cottage. The cottage seemed very quiet.

The robber crept in
through the back door.
"There's nothing here,"
he thought. "It's quiet and
it's dark. There's nothing here
at all."
Then he trod on the cat's tail.
"Hisssssssssssssssss!" The cat spat.
"Agh! A snake a snake!" screamed
the robber.

Hissssssssssssssssss!

Then the cat leapt up and
scratched the robber.
"It's a tiger! A tiger!" screamed
the robber.

21

The robber fell back onto the chair and sat on the dog.
The dog flashed his sharp white teeth.

SNAP!

It bit the robber on his bottom.

"A crocodile! A crocodile!" screamed the robber.

Then the rooster woke up and flew around the
room flapping his wings in the robber's face.
"An eagle! An eagle!" screamed the robber. He ran
to the front door ...where he fell over the donkey.

The donkey woke up and kicked.
He kicked the robber clean away.

Off flew the robber,

out of the room,

out of the cottage,

over the trees and far away.

The robbers were never seen again.

The donkey, the dog, the cat and the rooster still live in that cosy cottage. They have good food to eat, a warm fire to sit by, soft chairs and a good strong roof. Every morning when they wake up, they sing.

Every night, before they go to sleep, they sing some more.

They never did become rich and famous popstars – but they did live happily ever after.